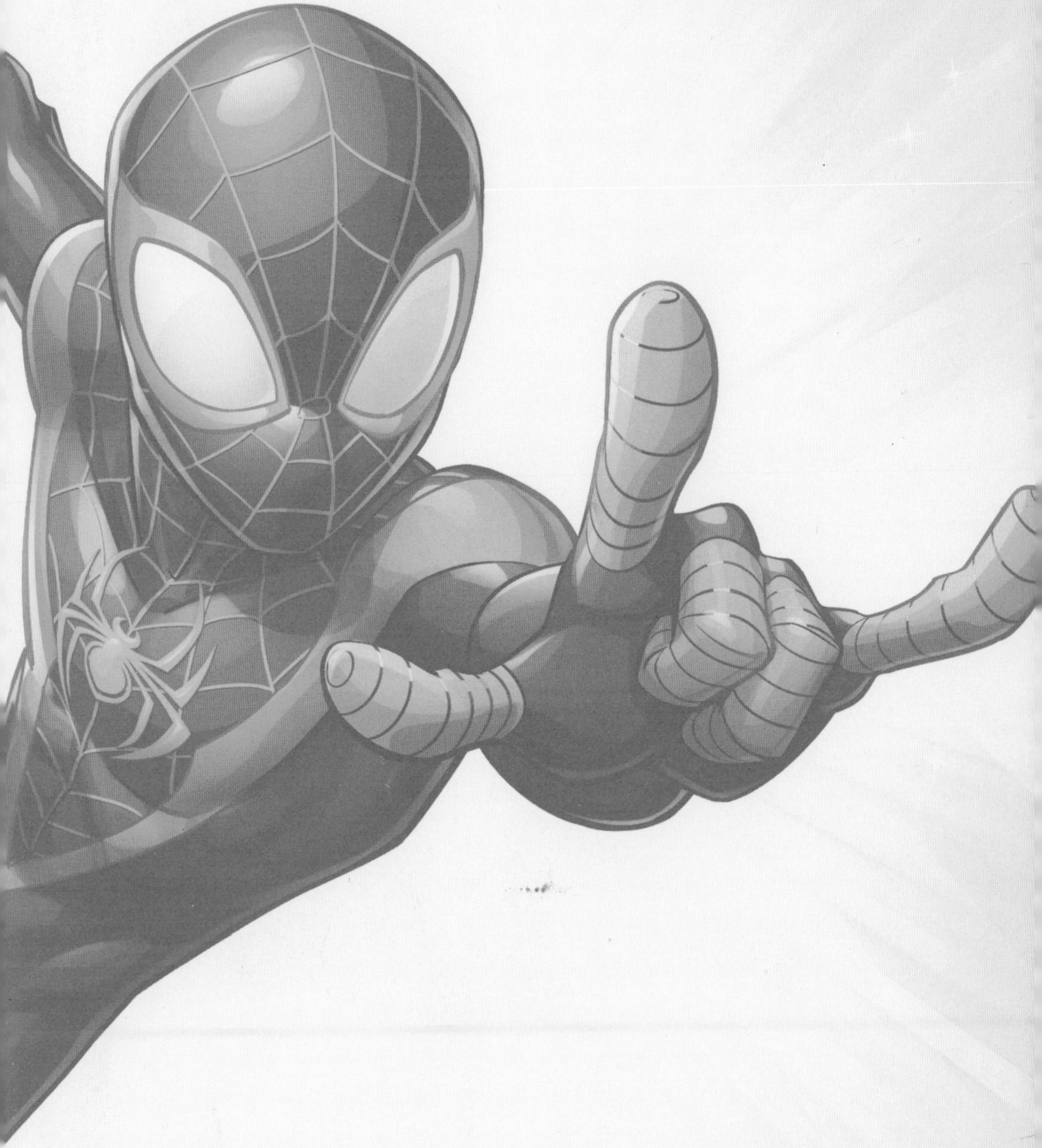

MARVEL
SPIDER-MAN

MILES MORALES
TO THE RESCUE!

Written by David Fentiman

DK | Penguin Random House

Senior Editor David Fentiman
Designer Stefan Georgiou
Production Editor Marc Staples
Senior Production Controller Louise Minihane
Managing Editor Sarah Harland
Managing Art Editor Vicky Short
Publisher Julie Ferris
Art Director Lisa Lanzarini
Publishing Director Mark Searle

Reading Consultant Dr. Barbara Marinak

First American Edition, 2021
Published in the United States by DK Publishing
1450 Broadway, Suite 801, New York, NY 10018

DK, a Division of Penguin Random House LLC
21 22 23 24 25 10 9 8 7 6 5 4 3 2 1
001–323478–Mar/2021

MARVEL

Published in Great Britain by Dorling Kindersley Limited.

A catalog record for this book is available from the Library of Congress.

ISBN: 978-0-7440-3716-6 (Paperback)
ISBN: 978-0-7440-3717-3 (Hardcover)

DK books are available at special discounts when purchased in bulk for sales promotions, premiums, fund-raising, or educational use. For details, contact:
DK Publishing Special Markets, 1450 Broadway, Suite 801, New York, NY 10018
SpecialSales@dk.com

Printed and bound in China

For the curious

www.dk.com

MIX
Paper from responsible sources
FSC™ C018179
FSC www.fsc.org

This book is made from Forest Stewardship Council™ certified paper—one small step in DK's commitment to a sustainable future.

Contents

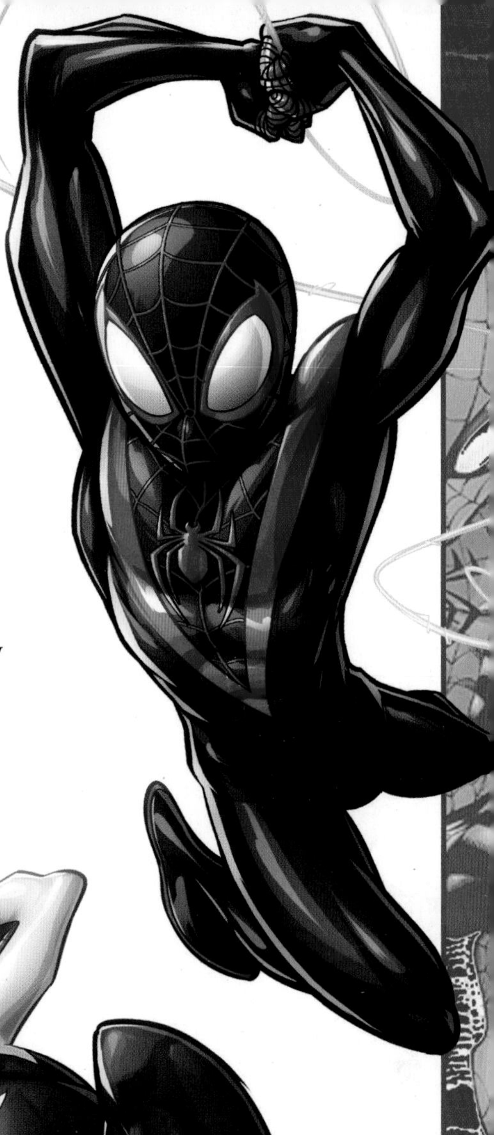

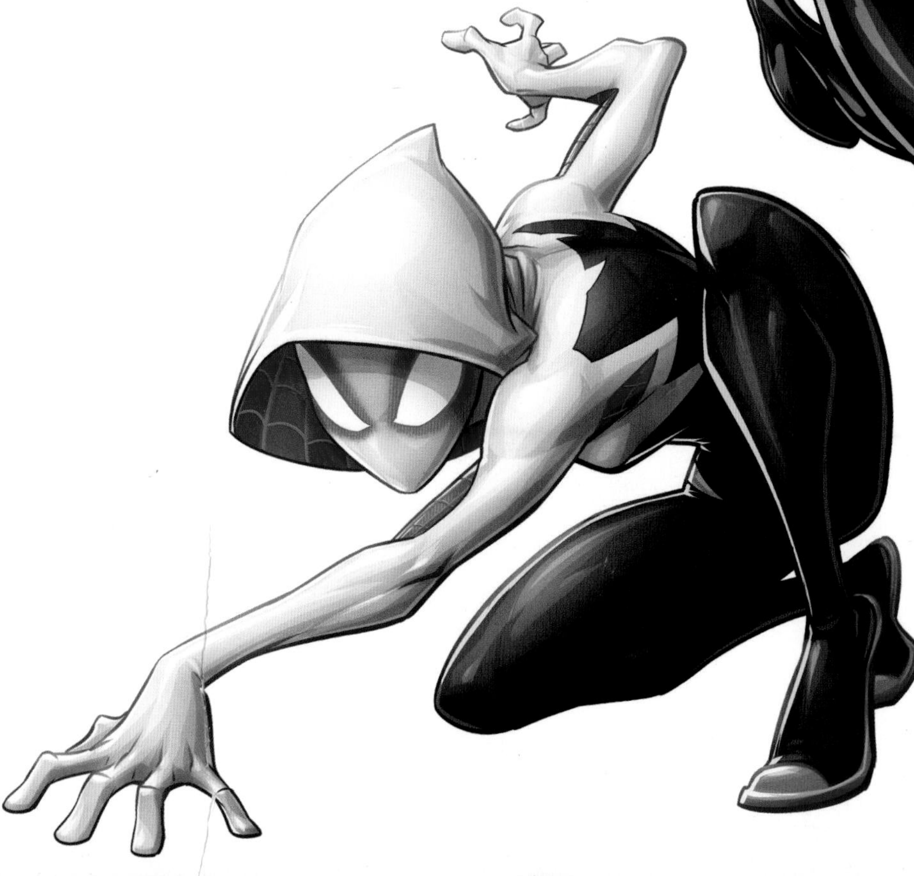

Meet Miles!

This is Miles Morales.
He lives in New York City.
Miles has a big secret!
He is really a Super Hero!

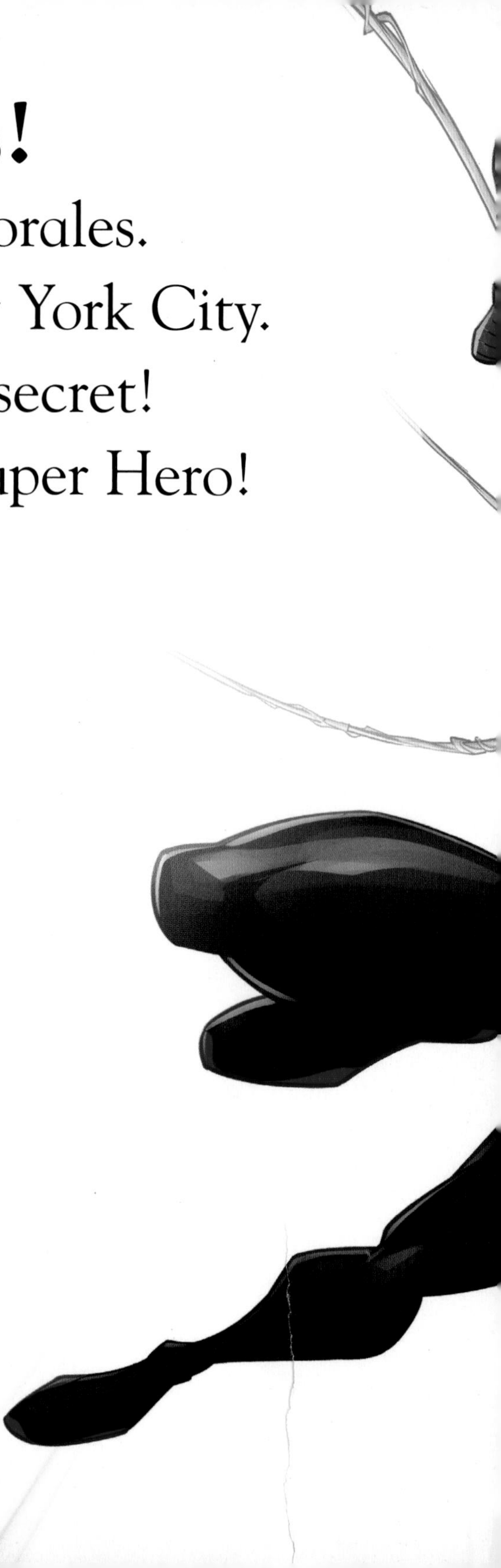

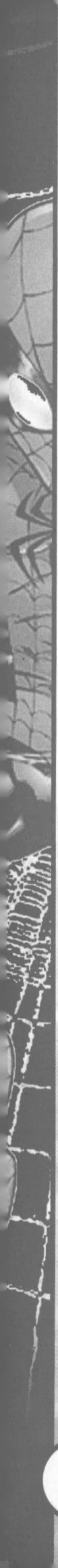

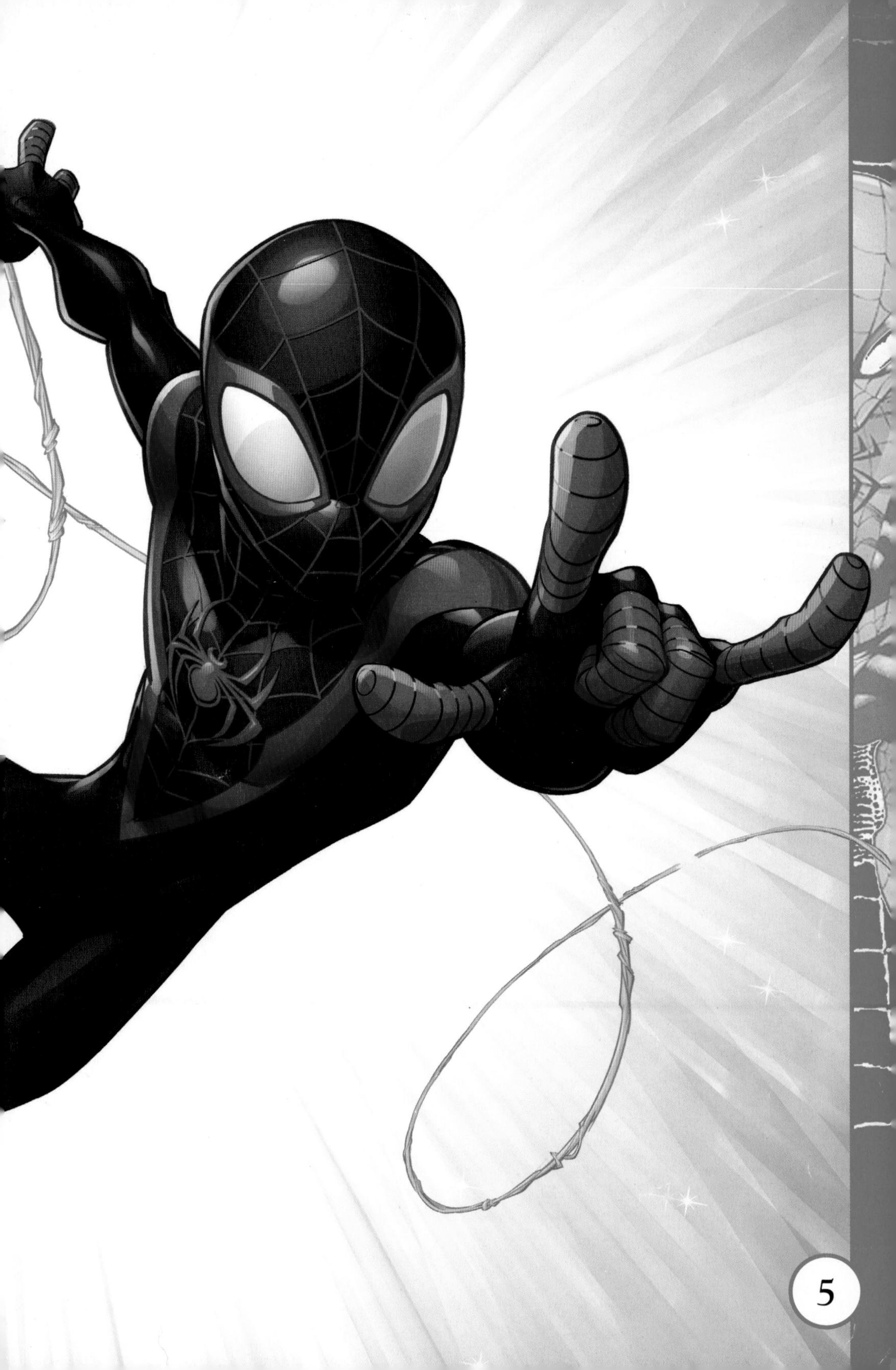

Spider-Powers

Miles got bitten by a spider.
The spider's bite gave him
lots of special powers.
Miles is now Spider-Man!

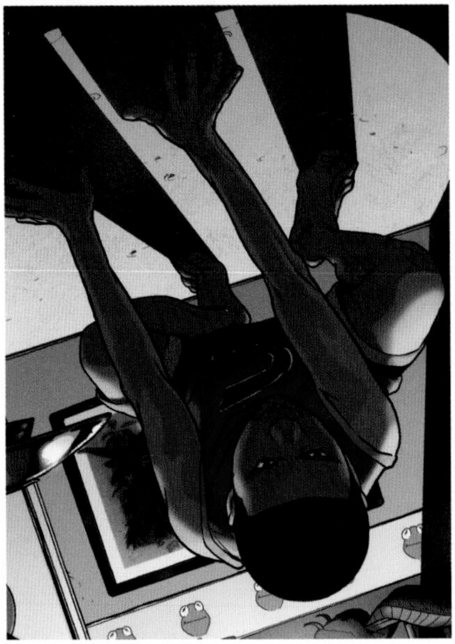

Miles can
climb walls!

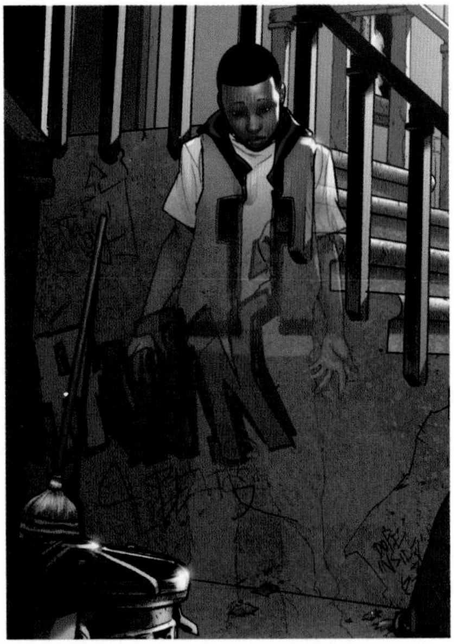

Miles can
hide himself!

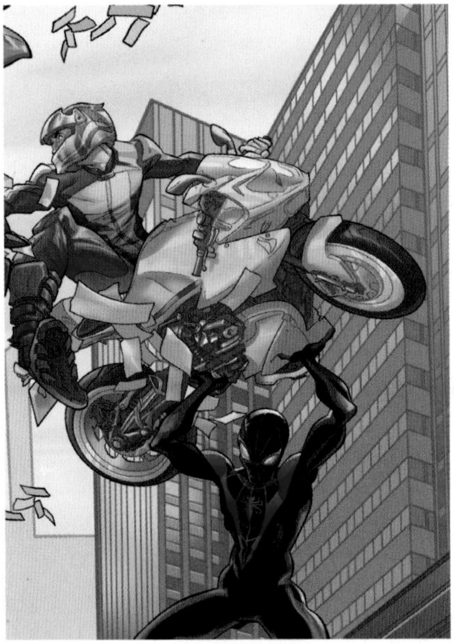

Miles is super strong!

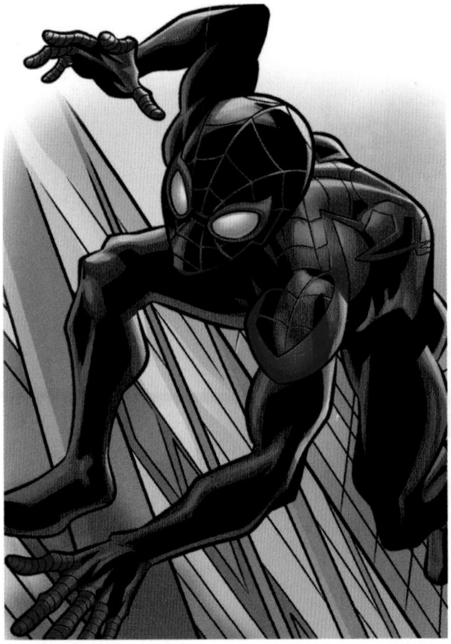

Miles is super fast!

Miles and Peter Parker

Miles is not the only Spider-Man.
Peter Parker is a Spider-Man too!
Peter was bitten by a special
spider just like Miles.
They battle crime together.

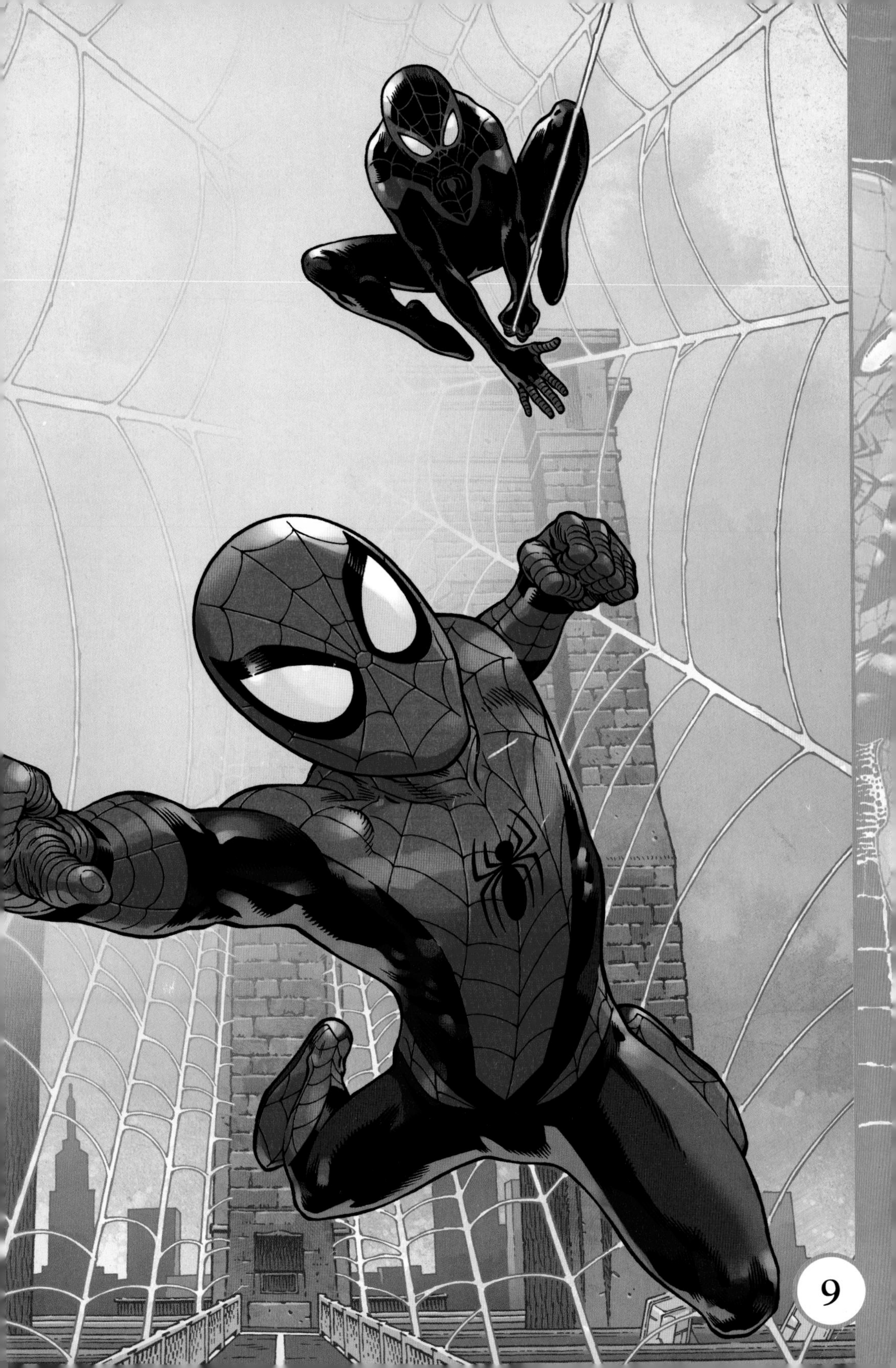

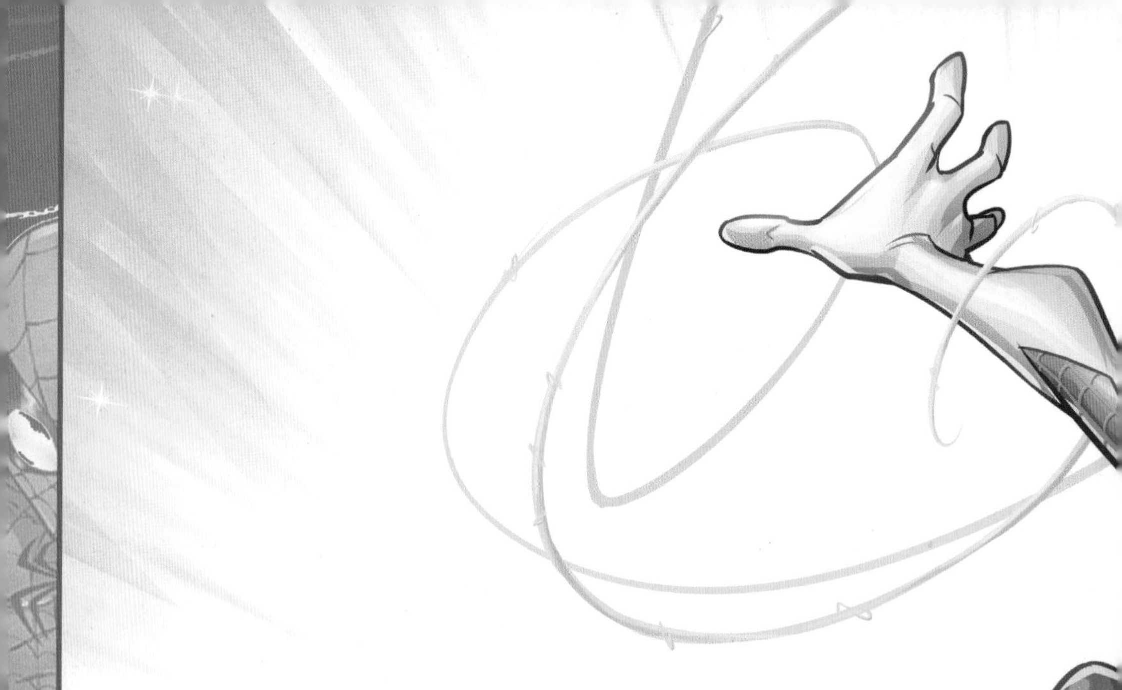

Ghost-Spider

Miles and Peter Parker are
not the only Spider-Heroes.
There are many others.
One of them is Gwen Stacy.
She calls herself Ghost-Spider!

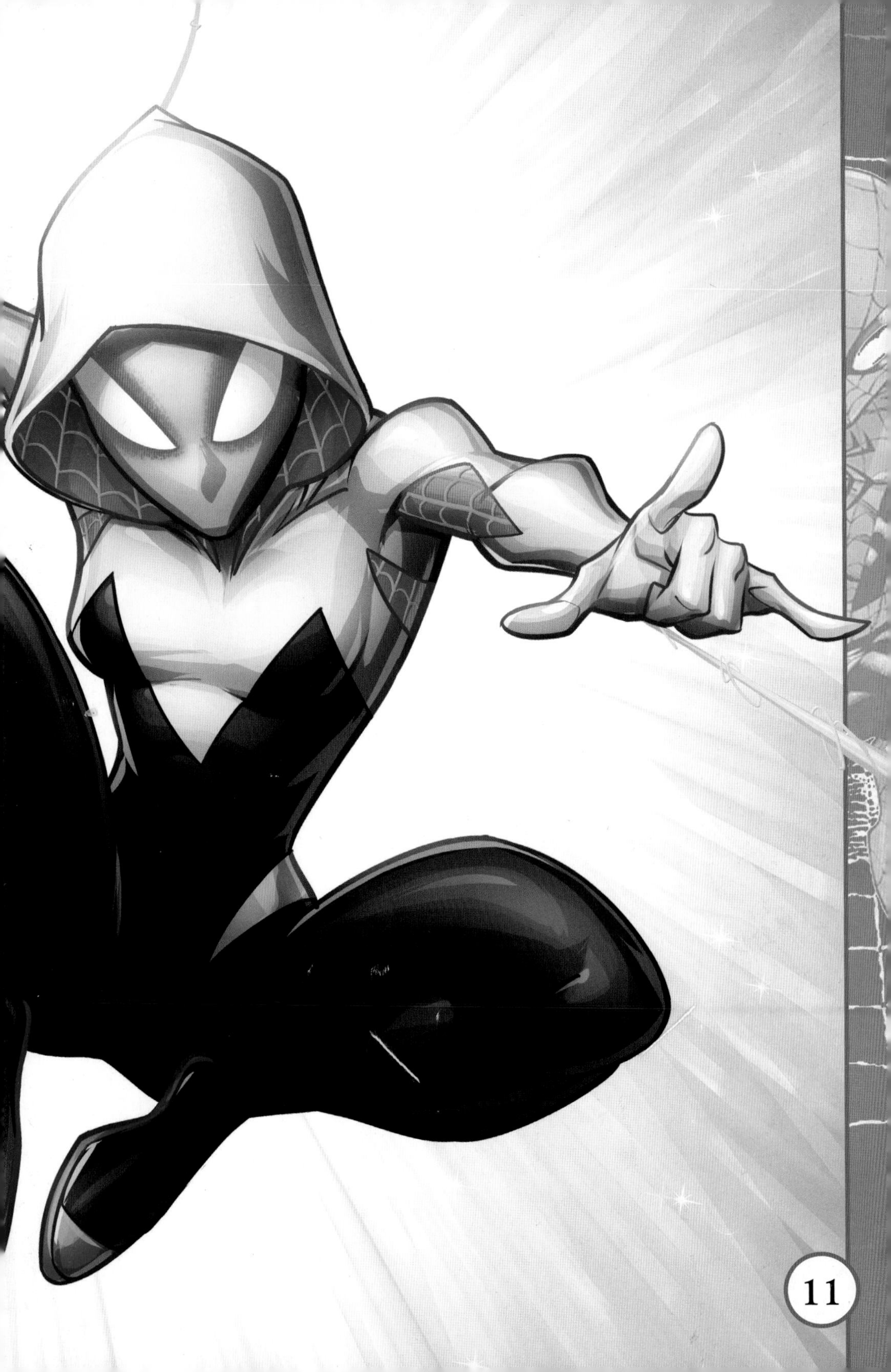

Miles in action

Miles shoots webs like a spider!
He can swing using his webs.
The webs are very strong.
Miles is not afraid of falling.

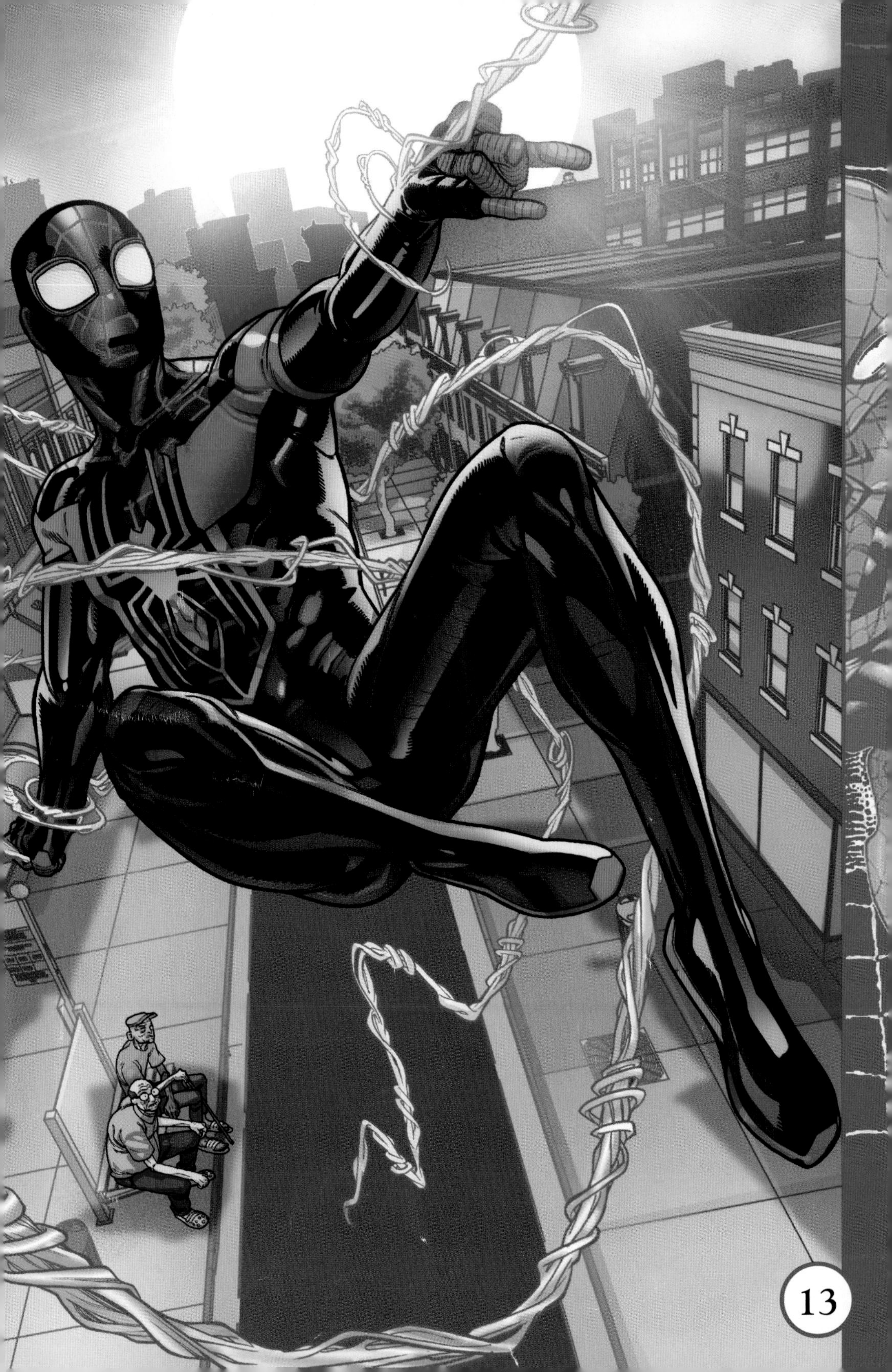

Miles' family

Miles lives with his parents.
Miles' mom is named Rio.
She is a nurse in the hospital.
Miles' dad is named Jefferson.
He is a police officer.

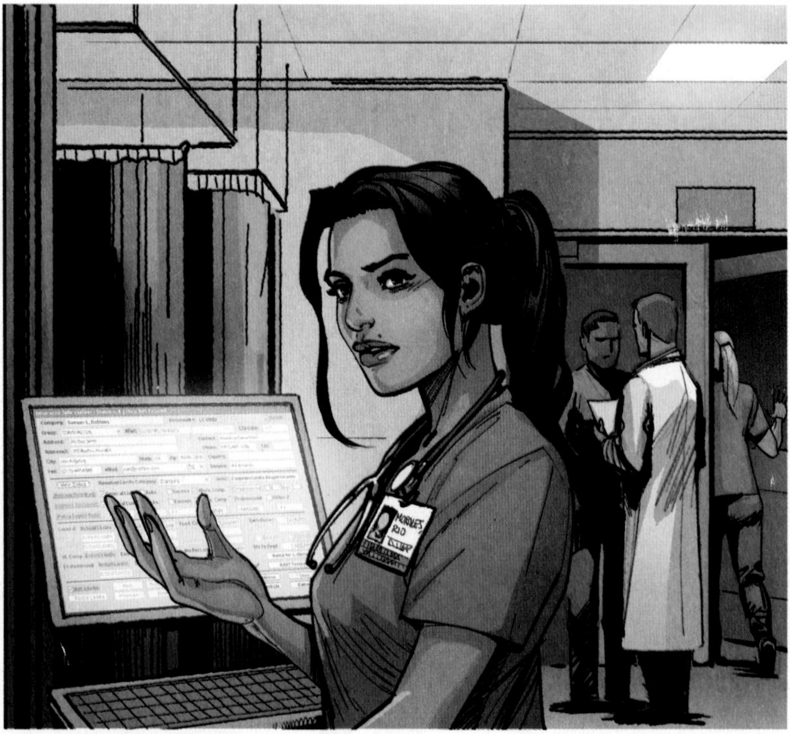
MORALES
RIO

Rio Morales

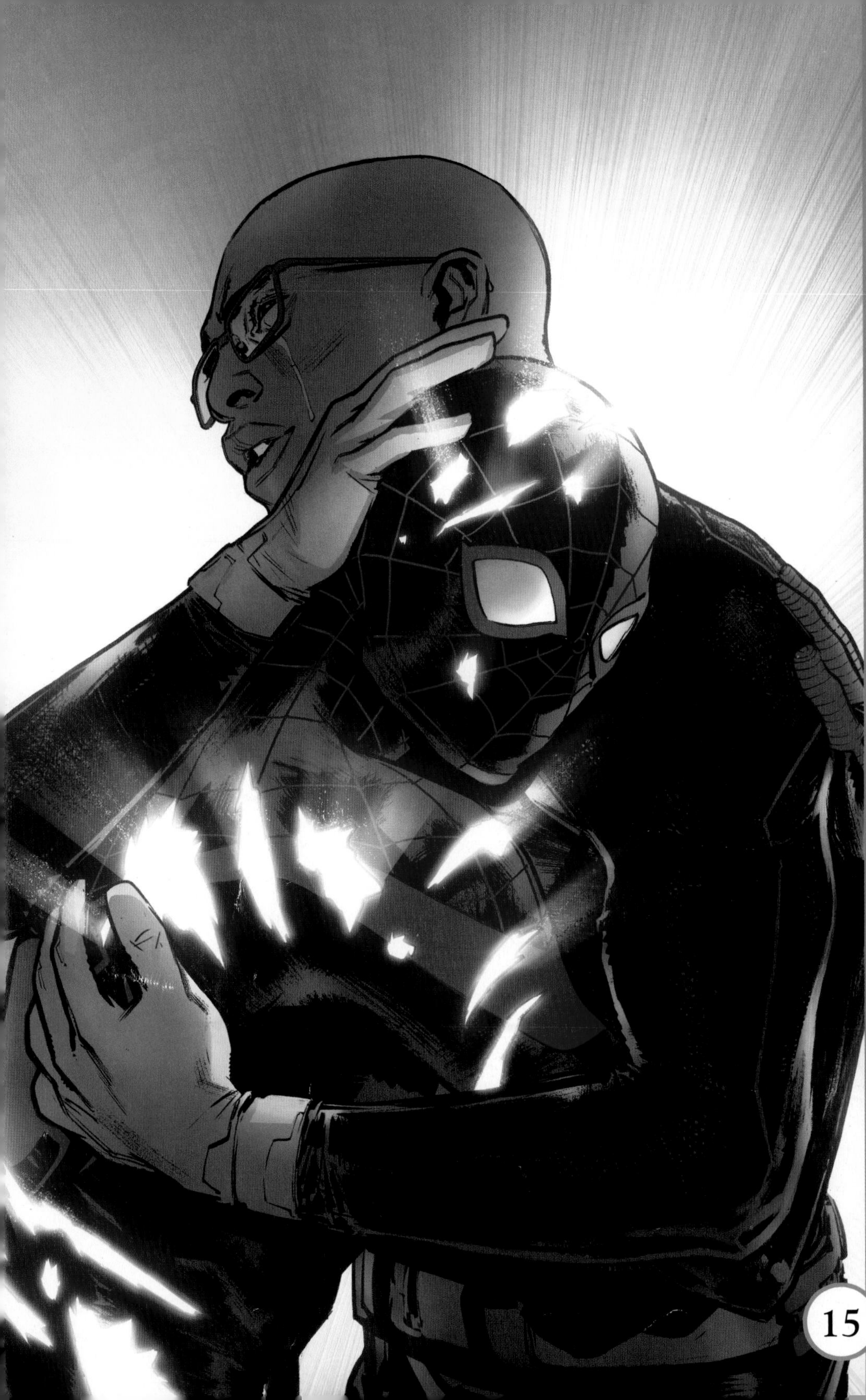

The Champions

Some of Miles' friends
are also Super Heroes!
They have made a team
called the Champions.
They all have special powers.

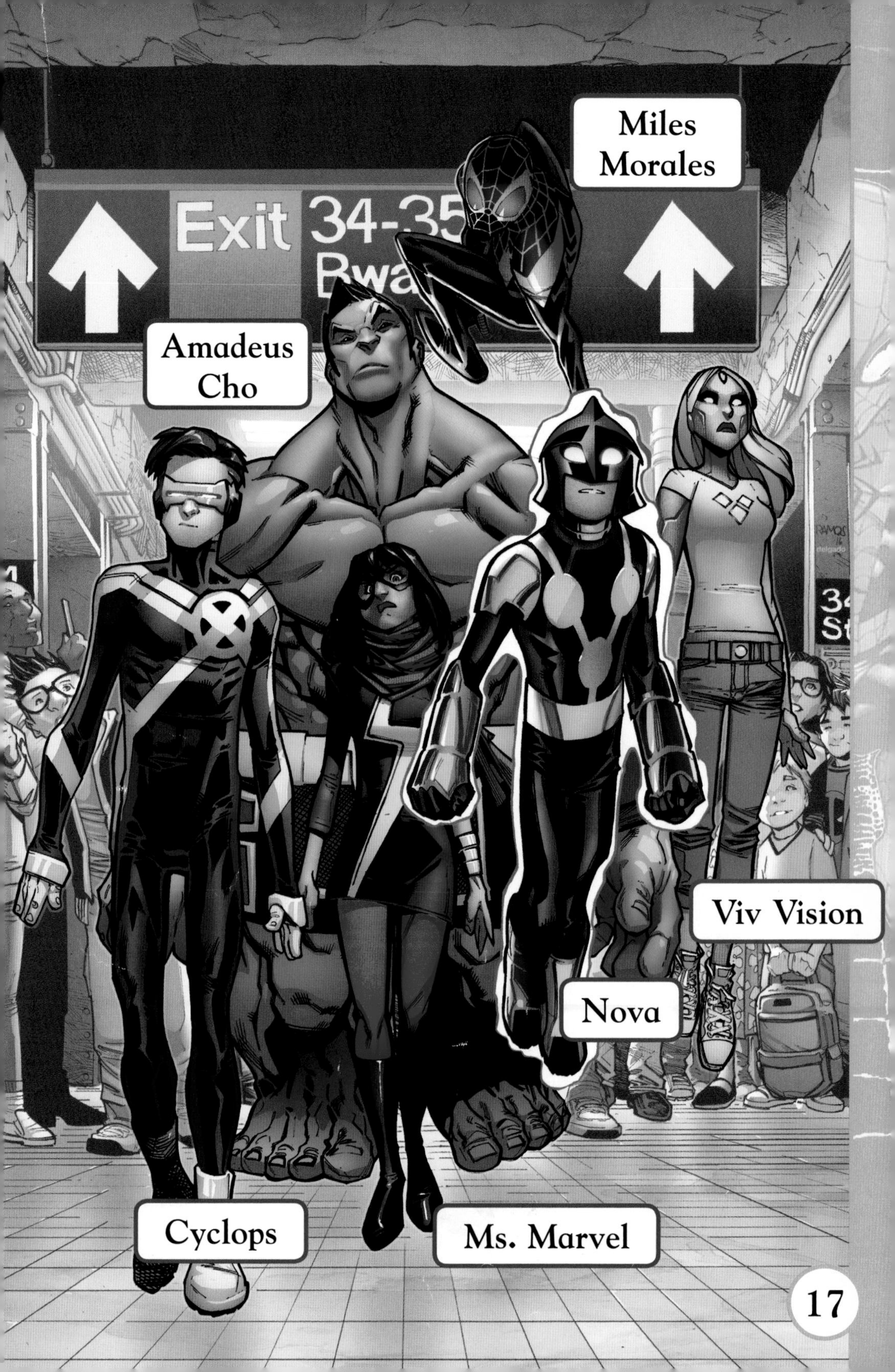
Exit 34-35
Bwa
Miles Morales
Amadeus Cho
Viv Vision
Nova
Cyclops
Ms. Marvel

The Sinister Six

The Sinister Six are bad guys.
They don't like Miles!

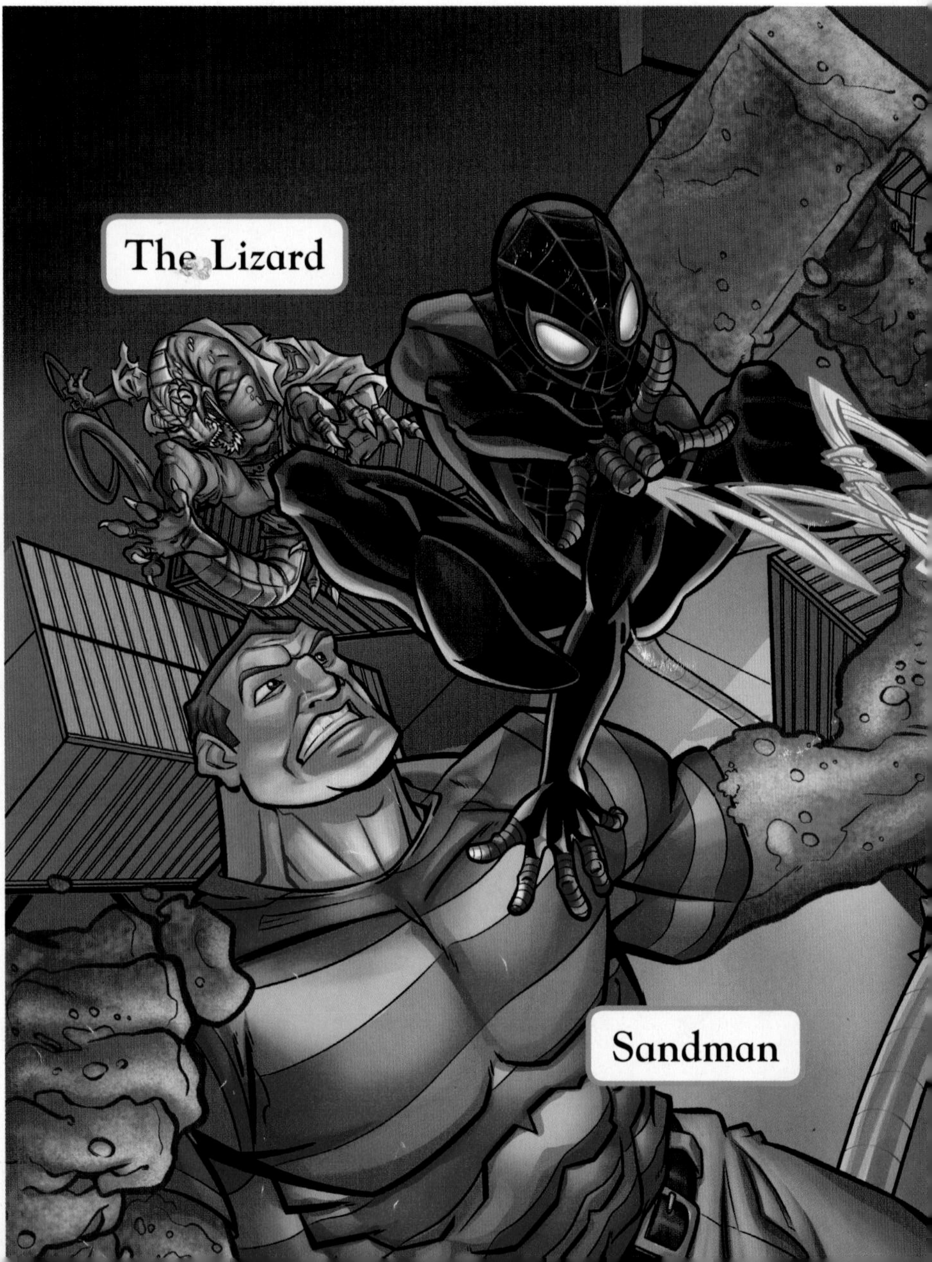
The Lizard
Sandman

They always try to defeat him. The Sinister Six want to take over New York City.

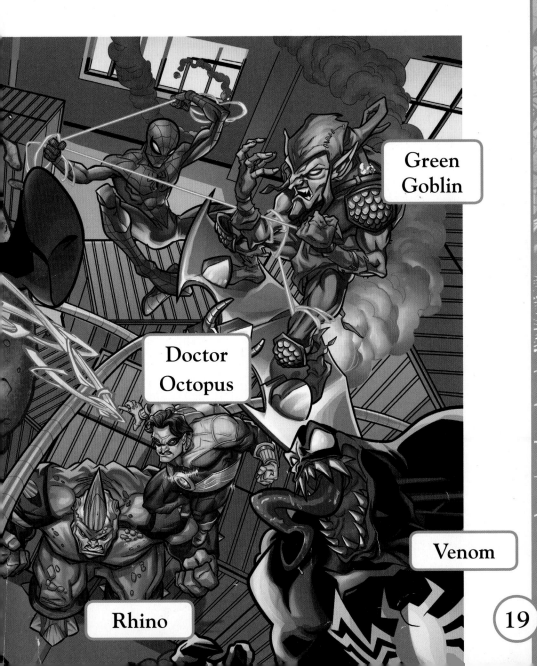

Green Goblin

Doctor Octopus

Venom

Rhino

Protector of New York City

Miles tries to keep his city safe. There are many bad people who want to hurt others. Miles must protect everyone.

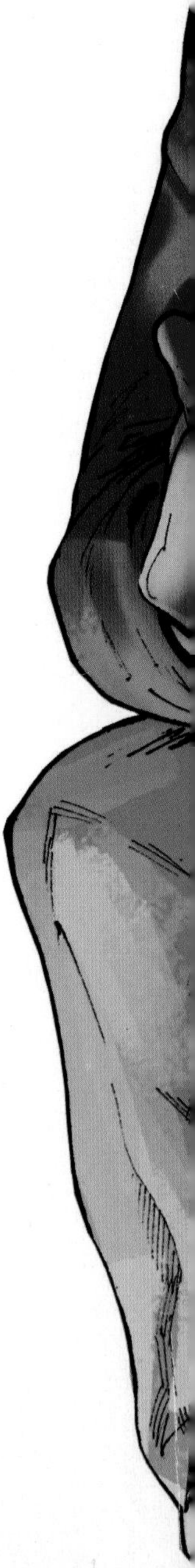

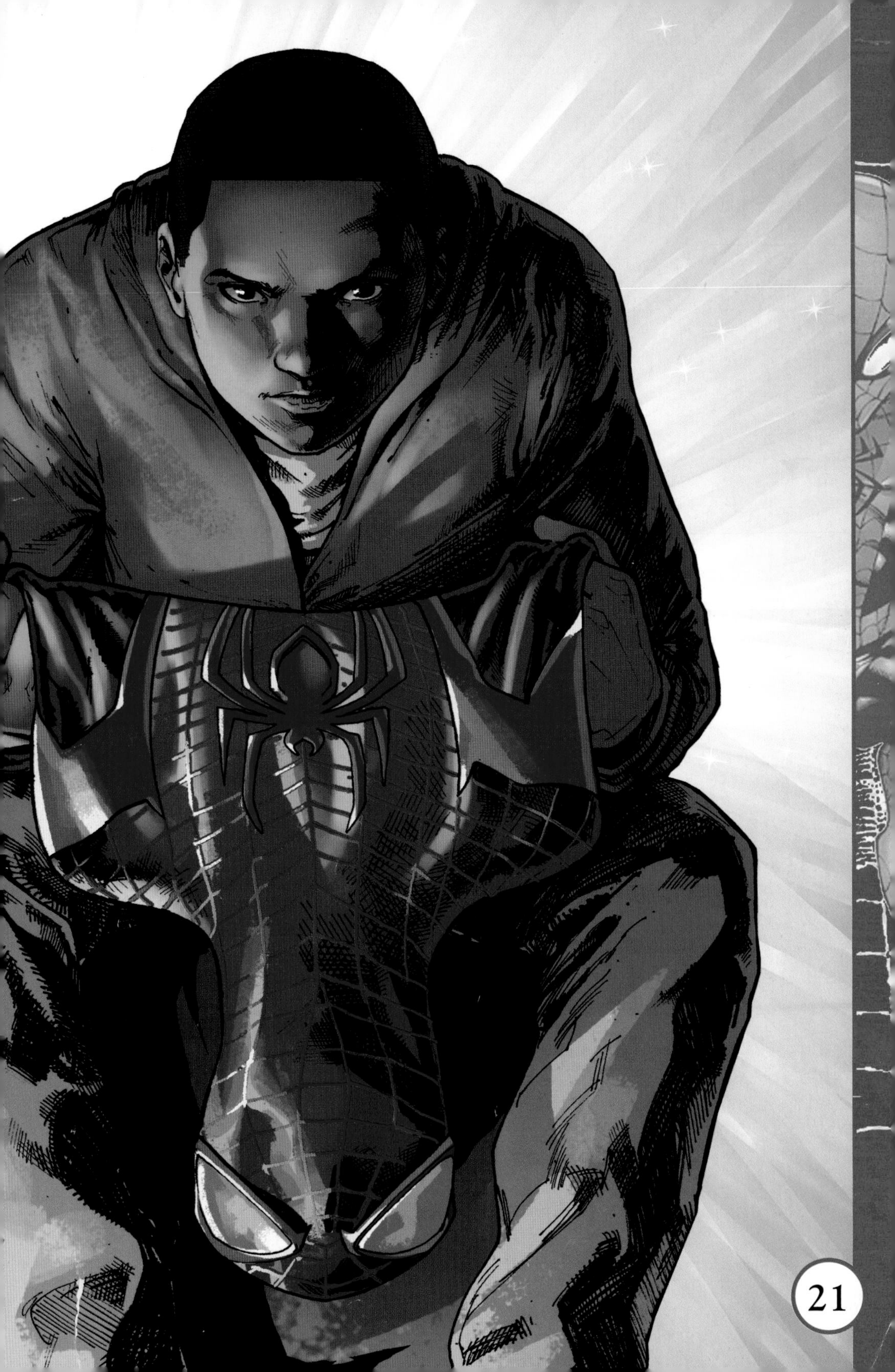

Quiz

1. Is Miles super strong?

2. What is Miles' last name?

3. How did Miles get his powers?

4. What is the name of the team Miles made with his friends?

5. Are the Sinister Six good or bad?

Index

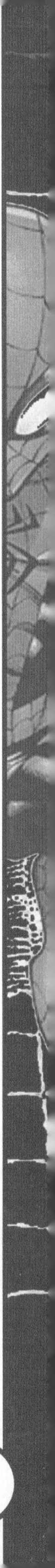

Answers to the quiz

1. Yes 2. Morales 3. He was bitten by a spider 4. The Champions 5. Bad

A LEVEL FOR EVERY READER

This book is a part of an exciting four-level reading series to support children in developing the habit of reading widely for both pleasure and information. Each book is designed to develop a child's reading skills, fluency, grammar awareness, and comprehension in order to build confidence and enjoyment when reading.

Ready for a Level 1 (Learning to Read) book
A child should:
- be familiar with most letters and sounds.
- understand how to blend sounds together to make words.
- have an awareness of syllables and rhyming sounds.

A valuable and shared reading experience
For many children, learning to read requires much effort, but adult participation can make reading both fun and easier. Here are a few tips on how to use this book with an early reader:

Check out the contents together:
- tell the child the book title and talk about what the book might be about.
- read about the book on the back cover and talk about the contents page to help heighten interest and expectation.
- chat about the pictures on each page.
- discuss new or difficult words.

Support the reader:
- give the book to the young reader to turn the pages.
- if the book seems too hard, support the child by sharing the reading task.

Talk at the end of each page:
- ask questions about the text and the meaning of the words used—this helps develop comprehension skills.
- read the quiz at the end of the book and encourage the reader to answer the questions, if necessary, by turning back to the relevant pages to find the answers.

Reading consultant: Dr. Barbara Marinak, Dean and Professor of Education at Mount St. Mary's University, Maryland.

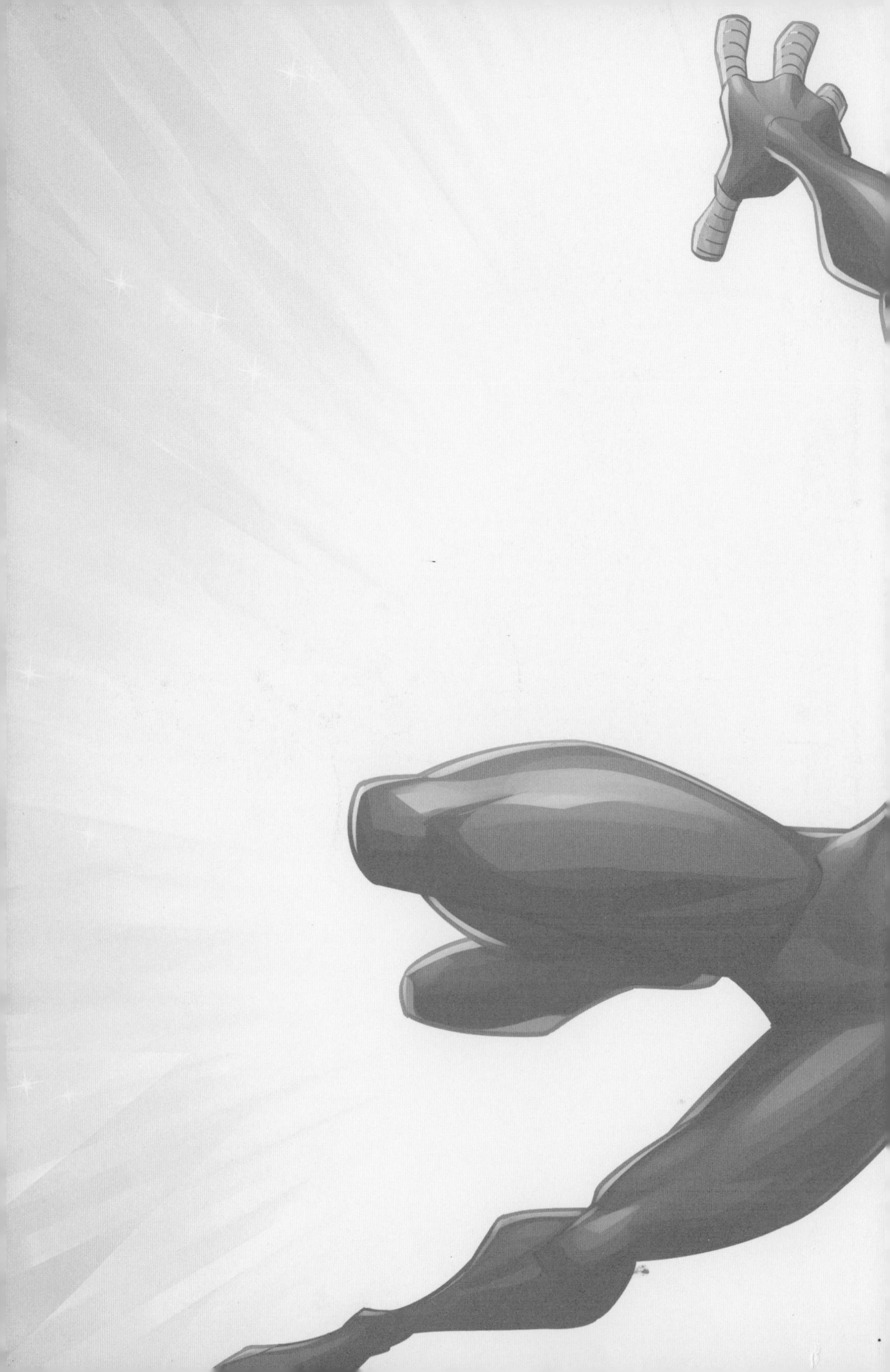